EDGARTOWN
Free Public Library

Presented by

CROCODILE
AND HEN

A Bakongo Folktale

CROCODILE

An I Can Read Book™

AND HEN

A Bakongo Folktale

TEXT BY JOAN M. LEXAU

PICTURES BY DOUG CUSHMAN

HARPERCOLLINSPUBLISHERS

This story is an adaptation of the tale entitled
"Why the Crocodile Does Not Eat the Hen"
from *Notes on the Folklore of the Fjort* by R. E. Dennet.
Courtesy The Folk-Lore Society, London.

HarperCollins®, 📖®, and I Can Read Book®
are trademarks of HarperCollins Publishers Inc.

Library of Congress Cataloging-in-Publication Data
Lexau, Joan M.
    Crocodile and hen : a Bakongo folktale / story by Joan M. Lexau ; pictures by Doug
Cushman.
    Adaptation of Why the crocodile does not eat the hen, from Notes on the folklore of the
Fjort (French Congo), by R. E. Dennet.
    Summary: Crocodile is so confused by Hen calling him "brother" every time he gets ready
to eat her that he finally goes searching for an explanation of how such a relationship can be.
    ISBN 0-06-028486-2 — ISBN 0-06-028487-0 (lib. bdg.)
    [1. Folklore—Africa.   2. Animals—Folklore.]   I. Cushman, Doug, ill.   II. Title.
PZ8.1.L45 Cr   2001   99-45410
398.2'096'798—dc21
[E]

1   2   3   4   5   6   7   8   9   10
❖
Newly Illustrated Edition

For Lucy Shanks
with love from GA Joan

To Ashley Bryan
for his friendship and inspiration
—D.C.

Day after day

Hen went down by the river

to look for food.

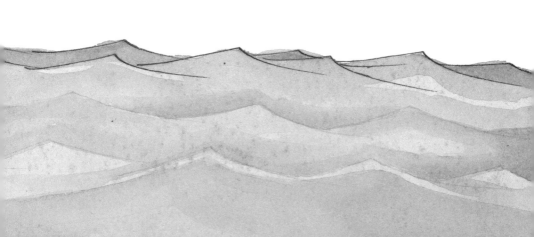

One day Crocodile saw Hen.

"I am going to eat you, Hen,"

said Crocodile.

He opened his mouth wide.

"My brother, don't eat me,"

said Hen.

She had so little fear of him

that she looked at him

with one eye.

She looked at him

with her other eye.

Then she looked away.

Crocodile shut his mouth,
SNAP!

He could not eat Hen.

He just could not do it.

He was so surprised at Hen

that he went on his way.

But then Crocodile said,

"Hen called me brother.

How can I be her brother?

How can she be my sister?

I am called Crocodile.

She is called Hen."

13

The next day

Hen went down by the river

to look for food.

Crocodile saw Hen.

"Now I am really

going to eat you, Hen,"

said Crocodile.

He opened his mouth wide.

"My brother, don't eat me,"
said Hen.
She had so little fear of him
that she shut her eyes
and fluffed up her feathers.

Crocodile shut his mouth,

SNAP!

He could not eat Hen.

He just could not do it.

He was so surprised at Hen

that he went on his way.

But then Crocodile said,

"How can I be Hen's brother?

How can Hen be my sister?

18

I am called Crocodile.

She is called Hen.

I live in water.

She lives on land."

19

The next day

Hen went down by the river

to look for food.

Crocodile saw Hen.

"Today I am really

going to eat you, Hen,"

said Crocodile.

He opened his mouth wide.

"My brother, don't eat me,"
said Hen.

She had so little fear of him
that she put her head down
for water.

She put her head back to drink it.

Crocodile shut his mouth,

SNAP!

He could not eat Hen.

He just could not do it.

He was so surprised at Hen

that he went on his way.

But then Crocodile said,

"How can I be Hen's brother?

How can Hen be my sister?

I am called Crocodile.

She is called Hen.

I live in water.

She lives on land.

I have fine scales all over me.

She has silly feathers all over her."

Crocodile went out of the water.

He walked on land.

As he walked, he said,

"I must ask the Wise Old Woman

about this."

Crocodile saw his friend Lizard.

Lizard said, "Friend,

why do you look so sad?

Can I help?"

Crocodile said,

"No, you can't help me.

I am sad about Hen.

She looks so fat and good to eat.

But when I am about to eat her,

she says, 'My brother, don't eat me.'

So I am on my way to ask

the Wise Old Woman about it."

"Hmmm," said Lizard.

Crocodile said,

"How can I be Hen's brother?

How can Hen be my sister?

I am called Crocodile.

She is called Hen.

32

I live in water.

She lives on land.

I have fine scales all over me.

She has silly feathers all over her."

"Hmmm," said Lizard.

"I said you can't help me,"

Crocodile said.

Lizard said,

"What do scales and feathers

and all that matter?

Don't ask the Wise Old Woman

about this, my friend.

You will just look silly."

"But—" said Crocodile.

"This must be it," Lizard said.

"Hen lays eggs.

Ducks lay eggs.

Turtles lay eggs.

Lizards lay eggs.

And *crocodiles* lay eggs.

We are all alike in this.

So in this way

we are brothers and sisters."

"I, Crocodile, am brother to Hen?

Hen is sister to me?"

asked Crocodile.

"Didn't Hen just say so?

Didn't I just say so?"

said Lizard.

"Oh, drat!" Crocodile said.

"That is too bad.

That fat, good-to-eat Hen."

The next day

Crocodile went to look for Hen.

He wanted to talk to her

as a brother should.

Crocodile saw Hen and he said,

"How good to eat you.

Oops, I mean *meet* you again,

Sister."

"It is always good to meet you,

Brother," said Hen.

And that is the way it was

ever after

with Crocodile and Hen.

Author's Note

Crocodile and Hen is based on a folktale from the Bakongo people of the Republic of the Congo, a country in west-central Africa roughly the size of the state of Montana. The Bakongo, also known as Kakongo or Fjort, live along the Congo River where it meets the Atlantic Ocean near the equator. This story is one of the wonderful old tales in the world that has been told by generation after generation of storytellers and that can be enjoyed by cultures everywhere.

I came upon R. E. Dennet's translation of "Why the Crocodile Does Not Eat the Hen" in *Notes on the Folklore of the Fjort* (published by the London Folk-Lore Society) years ago while I was researching folktales. As soon as I saw it, I loved this simple, humorous tale about a crocodile astonished by an unflappable hen. I still remember the pleasure I took in folktales when I first learned to read, and I was eager to adapt this one to share it with today's beginning readers.

—J.M.L.